A Dog's Best Friend

Written by Gare Thompson

Illustrated by John Magine

STECK-VAUGHN
C O M P A N Y
ELEMENTARY • SECONDARY • ADULT • LIBRARY

Contents

Meet Niles

Niles was a clever, young schnauzer.
He had soft gray hair brushed just right.
He had bright eyes and a friendly face.
He always smelled fresh and clean. Niles
was perfect!

He lived with his owner in a very big
apartment building in the city. Niles was
the only dog that lived in the building.
Everyone loved Niles. He was always on
his best behavior.

Every day, Niles and his owner went downstairs to go for a walk in the park. When someone new got on the elevator, Niles would sit up and raise his paw to shake hands. Everyone would pet Niles or give him treats. He would always bark "thank-you." Then Niles would prance beside his owner to the park.

Niles was very well behaved when he was in the park. He did not chase birds like other dogs did. He just pointed at them with his paw. Then his owner would watch the birds through her binoculars.

Niles played fetch with the children in the park. He could fetch sticks, balls, and even rocks. Niles liked being in the park.

On sunny days, Niles would lie down in the grass and soak up the sun. Then he would snooze away the whole afternoon. He enjoyed his peace and quiet.

Niles could also do tricks, such as rolling over or balancing a bone on his nose. He liked getting attention!

Crumley Moves In

Then one day, a new dog moved into the apartment next door to Niles. His name was Crumley. He was a big, messy basset hound. He was very clumsy. His ears dragged on the floor. And he smelled. Not bad, but just like any other ordinary dog.

11

Now when Niles stood quietly in the elevator, Crumley was right there. Crumley would bark and wobble all over the place. Everyone thought Crumley was cute. They gave him lots of treats. Some people even petted Crumley before Niles!

This made Niles mad. He tried to stay away from Crumley. Niles did not want to be Crumley's friend.

Niles Makes a Plan

Every night, Crumley made a lot
of noise. He barked at any little sound.
He bumped into things wherever he
walked. Because of Crumley, Niles could
not sleep. He missed his quiet nights.

Niles wondered how he could get
rid of Crumley. One night, an idea
came to him. This could be good-bye
to Crumley! Niles drifted off to sleep
with a smile on his face.

The next morning, Niles stood quietly in the elevator near Crumley. Niles silently chewed Crumley's leash. When Crumley began to run in the park, his leash would snap. Then he would run away!

Niles looked up and barked at his owner. He couldn't wait to get to the park.

At the park, Niles sat and waited.
Then Crumley ran after some birds.
Sure enough, Crumley's leash snapped.
Niles watched as Crumley ran out of
the park.

Later, Niles saw Crumley's owner
back at the apartment building. She
looked sad. Crumley really had run
away. This made Niles feel bad.

Niles Makes a Friend

Then there was a loud bark. It was Crumley! He came running down the sidewalk. He had found his way home. Niles couldn't believe it. Niles thought that Crumley must be smart after all.

The next day, Niles shook hands with Crumley. At the park, Niles showed him how to fetch and how to point at birds. Niles thought maybe Crumley could make a good friend.

Crumley thought Niles could make a good friend, too. Crumley showed him how to roll in the sand to stay cool. Crumley showed him how to splash in a puddle for fun. Crumley taught him how to find his way home by himself. Now Crumley and Niles liked being together.

After that day, Niles and Crumley were best friends. Niles was glad that Crumley had moved into the apartment building. They were going to have fun together.

STECK-VAUGHN

PAIR-IT BOOKS™

Pair-It Books™ provide beginning readers with
fiction and nonfiction on their favorite topics.

Early Fluency Stage 3

Pizza Pokey	Pizza for Everyone
Miss McKenzie Had a Farm	Farm Life Long Ago
The House That Jack's Friends Built	Animal Homes
Sky High	Hot Air Balloons
A Gift to Share	Gifts to Make
The Missing Pet	A Pet for You
The Lion and the Mouse	Lions
Freddy's Train Ride	Amazing Trains
Carlita Ropes the Twister	Storms!
Rain Forest Adventure	Inside a Rain Forest
A Dog's Best Friend	**A Look at Dogs**
The Crane Wife	Japan
How Spiders Got Eight Legs	A Look at Spiders
How the Rattlesnake Got Its Rattle	A Look at Snakes
Jenny and the Cornstalk	Corn: An American Indian Gift

Fluency Stage 4

My Prairie Summer	Laura Ingalls Wilder: An Author's Story
The School Mural	Diego Rivera: An Artist's Life
Timothy's Five-City Tour	Cities Around the World
Minerva's Dream	Gail Devers: A Runner's Dream
Milo's Great Invention	Inventors: Making Things Better
Why the Leopard Has Spots	Animals in Danger
Pignocchio	On With the Show!
Desert Treasure	Life in the Desert
The Voyage	Explorers: Searching for Adventure
Save the River!	Take Care of Our Earth

STECK-VAUGHN®
COMPANY
ELEMENTARY • SECONDARY • ADULT • LIBRARY

ISBN 0-8172-7274-7

9 780817 272746

O5-MAS-490